Hoppity-Hop

Alphabet Soup

A Phonics Reader

By Sasha Quinton

The Book Shop, Ltd.

New York, New York

Hoppity Frog needs a home.
His old **log** has turned to **rot.**

"Quick!" **sobs Frog.** "Before the **frost,**
I need to find another **spot.**"

Hoppity Frog hops into a **pond**.
Splish! Splash! **Splosh!** He swims **across.**

Plop!

Frog climbs up **on** the **soggy** bank.
He jumps into a bed **of moss.**

"This is **not** a special **spot!**"
So, **hoppity-hop, Frog** moves **along.**

"I will **cross** the world," says **Frog,**
"To find a **spot** where I **belong.**"

Frog climbs up a **long** blue rope.
He **hops** up **on** a **rock.**

Frog jumps inside a **pocket.**
It's cold **atop** an icy **block!**

Frog climbs **upon** a shiny **bottle.**
He sees a can and **pops** the **top.**

Frog hops into a puppy's dish.
Hoppity Frog just will **not stop!**

Frog jumps up **on** a **fox's** back.
He climbs an **orange** flower **pot.**

Frog even tries a cup of soup.
The soup inside is much too **hot!**

Tick, **tock.** The **clock** moves **on.**
Frog can't find where he **belongs.**

"I miss my **rotten log**," **Frog** sobs.
But then he hears some happy **songs.**

He **hoppity-hops** to the perfect **bog,**
And there he finds another **frog.**

RIBBIT!

RIBBIT!